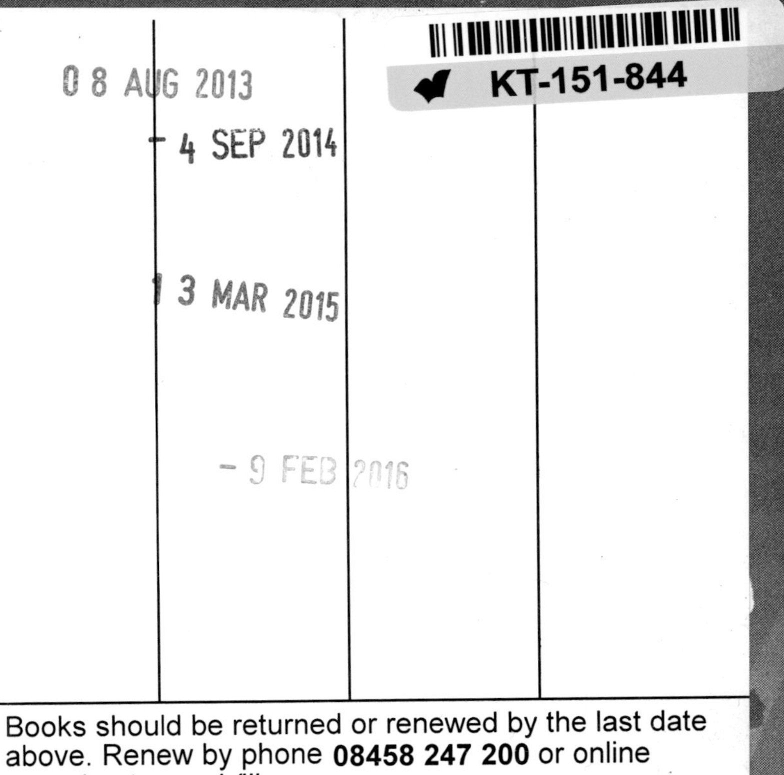

For Betty, Daisy, Max and Maisie
~ *GPJ*

STRIPES PUBLISHING
An imprint of Little Tiger Press
1 The Coda Centre, 189 Munster Road,
London SW6 6AW

A paperback original
First published in Great Britain in 2013

ISBN: 978-1-84715-379-1

A CIP catalogue record for this book is available from the British Library.

Printed and bound in the UK.

2 4 6 8 10 9 7 5 3 1

NINJA MEERKATS

THE FORBIDDEN PALACE

GARETH P. JONES

Oh, hello there. I heard a curious expression the other day.

"You can lead a horse to water, but you cannot make it drink."

What on earth does that mean? Why would I care if a horse drinks or not? I am not some kind of horse waiter.

In my experience, most animals will drink if they are thirsty. Even horses. If you are in the business of persuading horses to drink when they aren't thirsty, then I think you should seriously question what you are doing with your life. Maybe you should spend less time leading horses here and there and more time worrying about important things.

Four meerkats who concern themselves with the extremely important matter of keeping the world safe from the Ringmaster are the Clan of the Scorpion. Armed with deadly ninja know-how they are...

Jet Flashfeet: a super-fast ninja whose only fault is craving the glory he so richly deserves.

Bruce "the muscle" Willowhammer: the strongest of the gang, though in the brain race he lags somewhat behind.

Donnie Dragonjab: a brilliant mind, inventor and master of gadgets.

Chuck Cobracrusher: his clear leadership has saved the others' skins more times than I care to remember.

Oh, and me, Grandmaster One-Eye: as old and wise as the sand dunes themselves.

This story takes place in Peru, a country I know very well, having lived there once. So here's a song written by a Peruvian meerkat, Pam Pipes.

I once knew a goat from Peru
Who would chew and chew and chew.
When he chewed through a cable
Running under a table
His hair turned from white to bright blue.

Now, on with the story of...
THE FORBIDDEN PALACE.

CHAPTER ONE

PERIL IN PERU

The Clan of the Scorpion's underground base was different to most meerkat burrows. For instance, the walls were lined with swords, nunchucks, staffs and other fighting gear. Jet's kung-fu manuals and magazines lay scattered across the floor, and the main chamber was kitted out with all the latest modern technology, enabling the meerkats to keep in touch with the outside world.

Chuck, Donnie, Jet and Bruce were sitting cross-legged in front of their elderly mentor,

Grandmaster One-Eye, who had, yet again, fallen asleep in the middle of a sentence.

Jet sighed. "We're never going to learn how to perform the technique at this rate," he complained.

"What what what?" said Grandmaster One-Eye, waking up with a start.

"You're supposed to be teaching us the Flight of Enlightenment," said Jet. "Not falling asleep."

"You must have patience, young Flashfeet," said the old meerkat calmly.

"I'm starving. Is it lunchtime yet?" asked Bruce, shovelling a large slice of lizard cheese into his mouth.

"If you ask me, this move is impossible anyway," said Donnie.

"When one is truly in touch with one's inner ninja, impossible ceases to exist," said Grandmaster One-Eye. "Now please try to channel your *chi*."

"That's what I'm doing," said Bruce.

"No, you're *chomping* your *cheese*," sniggered Donnie.

"One must empty one's mind," continued Grandmaster One-Eye.

"Emptying Bruce's stomach would be more of a challenge," added Donnie.

"The Flight of Enlightenment is an ancient and mystical technique," said Grandmaster One-Eye. "One must sit cross-legged and reach an extreme meditative state. Then you must imagine you are standing at the other end of this chamber. Only once you can imagine success will you truly succeed."

"I'm imagining this lesson being over," muttered Donnie.

"The Flight of Enlightenment will propel you great distances with a gentle push," continued Grandmaster One-Eye. "But one must be completely relaxed first. Look at Chuck. He is in such a profoundly calm state that he has neither heard Donnie's jibes, nor Bruce's retorts, nor even Jet's complaints."

Their leader was sitting cross-legged with his eyes shut. He remained perfectly still, even when a loud ringing sound came from the computer console.

"That's an incoming call," said Donnie, leaping up and running to the console.

"Who is it?" asked Jet.

"It's Bruce's sister, Bella," replied Donnie.

"Bella!" exclaimed Chuck, suddenly springing to his feet.

"Hey, I thought you couldn't hear what we were saying?" said Jet.

"I had blocked out everything unimportant, but I've been waiting for this call," replied Chuck. He turned to

Grandmaster One-Eye. “I’m sorry, Grandmaster, but Bella Willowhammer has been trying to find out where the Ringmaster went after we lost him in the Australian Outback.”

“You must do what you must do,” said Grandmaster One-Eye, bowing graciously.

Donnie clicked a couple of buttons and a female meerkat wearing a large hat and coat appeared on one of the screens.

"Hey, Bella!" said Bruce.

"Hi, Bruce," she responded.

"Do you have news?" asked Chuck.

"Yes," replied Bella. "I've just heard that a man matching the Ringmaster's description chartered a flight this morning."

"Where was he heading?" asked Donnie.

"Peru. I intercepted the plane's transmissions and have discovered they will be landing in Cusco airport tomorrow morning."

"Peru?" said Jet. "Why Peru?"

"Perhaps he's taking a holiday," said Bruce. "It must be very tiring trying to take over the world all the time."

"I used to live in Peru, many years ago," said Grandmaster One-Eye.

"I wonder what he's up to," said Donnie, ignoring the grandmaster.

"I've started investigating that already,"

said Bella. “A recent earthquake in the mountains near Cusco has caused a landslide. It has revealed a path through the mountains. Locals believe that the path leads to the legendary Forbidden Palace.”

“The Forbidden Palace?” said Jet. “Sounds cool.”

“Unfortunately, I couldn’t find out much, except that the palace has lain undiscovered for so many centuries that most people believed it to be a myth. I’d love to help more, but I’ve got problems of my own. There’s a gang of pickpocketing possums in Perth to pursue.”

“The Clan of the Scorpion wishes you luck with your mission and thanks you for your help,” said Chuck.

“See you soon, sis,” said Bruce.

When Bella vanished from the screen, Donnie began busily typing away at the computer and scrolling through internet pages. "No one seems to know much about it," he said.

"The palace was built by the Incas," said Grandmaster One-Eye.

"What's an Inca?" asked Bruce.

"Hundreds of years ago, the Incas ruled Peru," said Chuck. "They were extremely powerful and devilishly inventive. How much do you know about this palace, Grandmaster?"

"I know that the world is in great danger if the Ringmaster finds it," said Grandmaster One-Eye.

"Why?" asked Jet.

"I can't exactly remember," Grandmaster One-Eye admitted. "As far as I recall, it was built for an Inca king who sought to gain Ultimate Power over the world. I'm afraid I forget the details...

But I can tell you someone who will not have forgotten. You must go and seek my old friend, the alpaca Señor Diego Citizen. He wears an ancient scroll around his neck, which reveals the palace's secrets. Now the way to the Forbidden Palace has appeared, he will be in great danger."

"Clan of the Scorpion, let us prepare." said Chuck. "We're going to Peru."

CHAPTER TWO

THE STOLEN SCROLL

Donnie used the journey to try out his latest suitcase disguise.

"I've replaced the pedals with a small motor," he said proudly. "Our days of walking or pedalling are over. Reclining seats, an in-case entertainment system and a fridge for Bruce's snacks. I don't even need to steer now I've fitted this computerized autopilot system. Sit back and enjoy the ride, my friends." He leaned back with his feet on the console and his hands behind his head.

Hidden inside the suitcase, the meerkats easily snuck on board a plane to Peru. However, a jolt from a particularly clumsy luggage handler when they arrived in Cusco caused something to go haywire. The suitcase scuttled off, zigzagging all over the place, crashing into passengers, airport staff and other luggage, while Donnie tried to bring it back under control.

In the end, the only solution was for Jet to smash the in-case computer with a powerful punch and for Chuck to cut a series of holes in the base. That way, the meerkats were able to walk the suitcase speedily outside before airport security caught up with them.

"I thought you said no more walking," Bruce complained.

"Well, there are still a few teething problems," admitted Donnie.

"This should remind us," said Chuck, "that the Way of the Scorpion teaches the importance of invention, but that our most powerful weapons come from within. Now let's ditch this disguise."

Dawn was breaking as the meerkats made their way to Señor Citizen's home. Even at such an early hour, Cusco was a busy, bustling sort of place, as stall owners

and street sellers prepared for the day. Finally, the meerkats reached Señor Citizen's home, high on a hill with a magnificent view of the city.

As the meerkats approached, an old shaggy-haired alpaca popped his head out. Around his neck was a scroll attached by a gold chain.

"*Amigos*," he called.

"What did he say?" asked Bruce.

"It means 'friends'," explained Donnie.

"I will give you one warning, *amigos*," continued the alpaca. "Turn around now and I will let you walk away with your lives."

"That doesn't sound very friendly," said Bruce.

"Señor Citizen, we mean you no harm," said Chuck.

"Harm? Hah!" scoffed Señor Citizen. "Four meerkats could no more harm the great Señor Diego Citizen than a flea could harm an elephant."

Jet laughed. "Do you know who we are?" he asked.

"*You* do not know who *you* are? That *is* worrying," said Señor Citizen. "Whoever you are, you will never get this scroll off me. This ancient document has been protected by my family for many generations. I will fight all of you at once if I have to."

"I could do with a bit of exercise after that long flight," said Bruce.

"We do not wish to fight you," stated Chuck.

"You should listen to your leader," said Señor Citizen. "He is right to be scared."

"Now, I didn't say I was scared," said Chuck quickly.

"The fear in your eyes is as clear as a fish in a mountain stream. Now, all of you prepare to fight the great Señor Citizen."

As the alpaca stepped out from his home, the meerkats saw that in place of his two back legs was a pair of large wooden wheels that squeaked as they rolled forward.

"I will now teach you the meaning of pain," he announced grandly, before charging down the hill towards them.

"Clan of the Scorpion, do not harm this alpaca," ordered Chuck.

"The Clan of the Scorpion?" Señor Citizen cried out, but it was too late to stop the momentum he had built up.

The meerkats jumped, dived and rolled out of his way as the wheeling alpaca went flying forward, losing control of his wheels and flipping right over. He landed on his back with his wheels spinning in the air and his front legs flailing.

“Where has everybody gone?” he asked, confused.

“We are right here,” said Chuck, as he and Bruce hauled the alpaca up.

“Thank you. I have heard of the Clan of the Scorpion,” said Señor Citizen. “Chuck Cobracrusher, the wise leader, Jet Flashfeet, the superfast ninja, Donnie Dragonjab, the inventor, and the powerhouse himself, Bruce Willowhammer. How is my old friend, One-Eye?”

“He is well,” said Chuck. “He suggested we contact you. You see, we suspect that the recent earthquake has revealed the location of the Forbidden Palace. If so, we have reason to believe that our arch-enemy seeks to use it to gain Ultimate Power. Is such a thing possible?”

“Allow me to tell you the legend of the Forbidden Palace,” said Señor Citizen.

"There were once two brothers. Both were Inca princes. The eldest was a very ambitious man, while the younger was extremely wise and clever. When the oldest brother became king he ordered his brother to construct a palace that would give him Ultimate Power. The younger brother spent several years building the palace, then handed his brother a scroll explaining how it worked. But then the king realized he had been tricked. You see, his brother never told him the location of the palace. In anger, the king threw his brother in prison."

"Did the king ever find the palace?" asked Jet.

"He did not."

"So, why is it called the Forbidden Palace?" asked Donnie.

"The king forbade anyone but him to enter," replied Señor Citizen. "He wouldn't even allow anyone to go with him as he searched for it, as he was fearful that they might claim the prize of Ultimate Power for themselves."

"And the instructions he carried are those that you now keep around your neck?" said Chuck.

"That is right, *amigo*. The king became hopelessly lost on his search, but before his death he met an alpaca high in the mountains. He gave this alpaca the scroll to keep safe. It has remained in my family ever since."

"The Ringmaster will try to get this scroll from you," said Chuck.

"Ringmaster?" exclaimed Señor Citizen. "Oh, I have already met a man by that name. He asked for the scroll but I refused to give it to him."

"When did he come here?" asked Bruce.

"Yesterday."

"Who was with him?" asked Chuck.

"There was this Ringmaster of yours, his pet dog, a man with many knives, two gentlemen with painted faces and a local man known as the Birdman of Cusco."

"The Birdman of Cusco?" said Donnie.

"Yes. He is a strange fellow. He wears a cloak of feathers and they say he has a whistle that gives him power over all birds."

"And these goons didn't try to get the scroll by force?" asked Jet.

"They didn't dare take on the great Señor Diego Citizen."

The meerkats looked at the old alpaca doubtfully.

"They put on a show for me. It wasn't any good. The two painted-face men did some very unfunny falling over and some rather poor juggling. Then they left."

"And you kept the scroll with you at all times?" said Donnie.

"Yes..." Señor Citizen paused thoughtfully. "Except when the painted men asked to use it for juggling. Apparently they had forgotten one of their juggling sticks. They were not very good at it and kept dropping the sticks, but they gave the scroll back when they finished."

Chuck's expression changed to one of deep concern. "Señor Citizen, have you checked the scroll since the show?"

"No."

"Please, do so now," urged Chuck.

Señor Citizen unravelled the scroll and gasped. "What is this trickery? Look, *amigos*."

Scrawled on the scroll were the words: "Knock knock. *Who's there?* Inca. *Inca who?* In case you're wondering, we've got the scroll!"

"This is a catastrophe," wailed Señor Citizen.

"It's certainly a pretty bad joke," said Donnie.

"It seems that the clowns switched your scroll for this fake one," said Chuck.

"But if they have the scroll then they will have read the instructions," said Señor Citizen. "They'll be on their way to the Forbidden Palace now."

"What exactly does the true scroll say?" asked Chuck.

"It contains a rhyme about how the palace works," said Señor Citizen. "*He who seeks Ultimate Power must sit upon the golden throne, so when the sun shines upon him, the earth shall be his own.*"

"The palace must have magical powers," said Jet.

"The brother who built it was a great engineer and a wise thinker, but I have never heard that he was a magician," said

Señor Citizen. "What will happen now your Ringmaster has the scroll? I have spent my life guarding it. I have failed!"

"We've stopped the Ringmaster before and we'll do so again," said Chuck.

"You must take the path across the mountains," said Señor Citizen. "The Forbidden Palace lies beyond Mount Waytusteep. The earthquake revealed a passage through the great mountain. I would join you, too, but unlike my hind legs, my trekking days are behind me."

"Surely the Ringmaster will use his hot-air balloon to reach the palace," said Donnie.

"No," said Señor Citizen. "The winds are very strong up in the mountains. Only birds can navigate those air currents."

"But if it was never found, how do we even know that this place is the real

Forbidden Palace?" asked Donnie.

"You will know by its surroundings," replied Señor Citizen. "Legend tells of how the real Forbidden Palace is surrounded by a vast marsh of slow-sinking mud."

"Slow-sinking mud? What's that?" asked Bruce.

"It is a kind of mud that, if you land in it, will drag you down into the belly of the earth. You certainly wouldn't want to land a hot-air balloon in it. The Ringmaster will have no choice but to trek over the mountains and cross the mud by the stepping-stone path."

"Then that is what we must also do," said Chuck.

"Beware this Birdman your Ringmaster has recruited," warned Señor Citizen. "He is a sly old bird."

"Don't worry. He'll be spitting feathers by the time we're through with him," said Jet.

AERIAL ATTACK

The sun was still creeping up in the sky when the meerkats set off on the trek to the Forbidden Palace, following the path that snaked over the tree-covered mountains.

At the top of the first mountain, Chuck paused to survey the horizon. "The Ringmaster has a day's head start. We must move quickly if we are to catch up with him."

"I've got just the thing," said Donnie. From inside his rucksack, he pulled out a small glider with two fold-out wings. It had a bar at the front for Donnie to steer and one at the back for the other three to hang on.

"It's my new meerkite," said Donnie. "We may not be able to fly all the way to the palace, but we should be able to use it to catch up with the Ringmaster."

"Very good," said Chuck.

"You'll all need to put these on," said Donnie, handing out parachutes to the others. "With these strong mountain winds, landing the meerkite will be tricky. It'll be easier to skydive down. Now, hold on tight and when I say run, RUN."

"When you say run, run, what?" asked Bruce.

"Run," replied Donnie.

"When you say run, run, RUN?" said Bruce.

"What, run? Now?" said Jet. "OK."

Jet charged towards a steep drop,

meaning the others also had to start running, too. At the edge they all jumped and the meerkite took to the air. For a hair-raising moment it felt like it was going to drop like a stone, but a strong breeze caught the meerkite and sent it flying forward, whizzing over the spectacular view.

They all kept their eyes out for signs of the Ringmaster but it was not easy from such a height. Finally, Chuck spotted something. “Donnie, there’s a speck of colour in amongst the trees down there,” he said.

Donnie angled the meerkite and flew over the area Chuck was pointing out. Sure enough, there amongst the green of the trees was a line of people dressed in brightly coloured clothes.

“It must be them,” said Jet.

“OK. You three parachute down,” said Donnie. “I’ll have to fold up the meerkite before I release my parachute but I’ll be right behind you.”

“Very good,” said Chuck. “Clan of the Scorpion, let’s drop in on our old enemy.”

Donnie watched as the others let go and then released their parachutes, falling silently towards their target.

He pressed the button to fold up the meerkite but nothing happened. He felt a sudden jolt and looked up to see two claws sticking through the meerkite. As the claws tore through the material he could see that they belonged to a ferocious-looking condor with huge wings and a large pointed beak.

"Hey, buzz off, beaky," yelled Donnie.

The condor squawked in reply and flapped its wings, carrying the meerkite upwards and taking Donnie with it, away from the others.

"As much as I like a good fight, I might just drop out of this one," said Donnie.

He released his grip on the meerkite but the bird saw what he was doing, tossed the tattered meerkite to one side then dived after him.

"Going down, eh?" said Donnie.

He waited until the condor was almost upon him then pulled the cord on his parachute. It opened and slowed him down so much that the condor went hurtling past him. But as it did so, the condor caught the parachute in its claws.

Suddenly, Donnie found himself speeding up, as the parachute flapped and fluttered uselessly behind him.

As he spiralled down towards the earth at great speed, Donnie felt a tug. The condor had flown back up and sunk its talons into his backpack. It was carrying him away.

Donnie struggled but the grip of the bird's claws was firm. "Great, I've been bird-napped!" he muttered. "Hey guys!" he yelled – but the others were too far away to hear. He wasn't even able to reach his phone to call them.

Chuck, Jet and Bruce steered towards the circus troupe, as unaware of Donnie's trouble as the Ringmaster was of them.

The Ringmaster led the way, with Doris the dancing dog by his side. Following him were the clowns, Sheffield and Grimsby, Herr Flick the knife-thrower, and a man wearing a cloak made from brightly coloured feathers with a hood shaped like a bird's head.

"Do you think that's the Birdman of Cusco?" asked Bruce.

"Either that or he's on his way to a fancy-dress party," said Jet.

"Quiet," scolded Chuck. "The element of surprise is the best weapon we possess."

The meerkats were close to the ground when the squawk of a bird made Doris look up and start barking.

"The Clan of the Scorpion," shouted the Ringmaster. "Get them!"

Herr Flick drew several knives from his belt and threw them. The meerkats dodged the blades but the knives tore through the fabric of their parachutes, causing them to lose control and crash to the ground.

"Circus acts, get these meerkats," ordered the Ringmaster, cracking his whip. "I will not allow them to get in my way this time."

"Like a traffic light stuck on red, we are

here to stop you," countered Chuck, springing up on to the branch of a tree and drawing his sword.

The Ringmaster cracked his whip at him, but Chuck leaped over it and landed back on the branch with perfect balance.

"Herr Flick, cut him out of the equation," ordered the Ringmaster.

The evil knife-thrower attacked, but Chuck drew his sword and sent the knives pinging off in all directions before jumping down to the ground.

"Doris, the floor is yours," shouted the Ringmaster.

Doris moved towards Chuck with a sinister salsa. She jumped up and performed a magnificent backflip and a powerful snap kick. Chuck skilfully dodged out of the way, before sending the dastardly dog reeling with a blow of his own.

Bruce and Jet were facing the clowns, who were both wielding strange-looking guns.

"Eh up, Grimsby," said Sheffield, "I don't remember inviting these two to the party."

"Nor me, but it would be rude to let them go without having some cake," replied Grimsby.

"Cake? I'm starving," said Bruce.

"Well, eat this then." Sheffield squeezed the trigger, sending a stream of gunky mess

from the barrel of his gun.

Jet dived out of the way but Bruce was too excited by the prospect of cake and the mixture covered him from head to toe.

"Now for the icing," said Grimsby. He pulled the trigger of his gun and white goo shot out, coating Bruce until all that was left was a Bruce-shaped mound.

"Hah," said Grimsby. "That's super-quick-setting cake mix and reinforced cement icing. No one can get out of–"

But before he could finish his sentence, cracks had appeared in the icing and Bruce burst out, sending shards of icing flying in all directions. He bent down to pick a lump of cake mix off the floor and took a bite. "Mmm, not bad. Needs more sugar," he said. "Now, where were we?"

"We were about to break up this party," said Jet. "Ninja-boom!" He leaped up at Grimsby and kicked him squarely in the chest, sending him staggering back.

Bruce jumped up and came down hard on Sheffield's foot.

"Youch," cried the clown, hopping away.

"You useless clowns," yelled the Ringmaster. "But my newest recruit will ruffle your feathers, meerkats."

The Birdman of Cusco nodded silently, then dramatically swirled around and stretched his arms out wide. Suddenly, from inside his cloak a flock of colourful birds flew out towards Bruce, Jet and Chuck.

The meerkats ducked to avoid being jabbed by their beaks but the birds fluttered around them, squawking and pecking at them aggressively.

By the time Chuck had seen them off with his sword, the Ringmaster and his troupe had gone.

"Come on. We'll catch them up soon enough," said Jet.

"Hold on," said Chuck, "Where's Donnie?"

Above their heads, they heard a distant squawk.

"Look," cried Bruce, pointing into the sky.

A large bird was flying up towards the mountain peaks, carrying with it something distinctly Donnie-shaped.

CHAPTER FOUR

KNOCKOUT POOP

Jet got no reply from Donnie's mobile, but Chuck remembered Donnie had fitted them all with tracking devices. When he accessed the map on his own phone, they could see three small red dots huddled together.

"This must be us," said Bruce.

"And that must be Donnie," said Jet.

Donnie's dot was moving away rapidly.

"That bird is taking him towards Mount Waytusteep," said Chuck. "This must be the Birdman's doing."

"Well, he's messing with the wrong

meerkats if he thinks he can get away with kidnapping Donnie," said Jet.

"We need to rescue him!" said Bruce.

"We must continue after the Ringmaster first, and then help Donnie," said Chuck. "But keep your eyes on the skies. We cannot afford any further losses."

On foot now, the meerkats followed the trail through the forest and out into the bright sunlight, where they got a brief glimpse of the Ringmaster and his troupe hurrying along the path.

"This is when Donnie would produce some kind of super-speedy skateboard to help us catch up," said Jet.

"Or rocket-fuelled roller skates," added Bruce.

Chuck nodded. "As it is, we will have to rely on our ninja training and natural speed."

They followed the path up a steep incline for several minutes, moving as fast as their legs would carry them. But as they gained height, it became more difficult to breathe.

"I don't feel well," said Bruce.

"You are experiencing altitude sickness," said Chuck. "It is normal to feel sick and dizzy up in the mountains."

"Is it normal to see things that aren't there?" asked Bruce.

"I don't think so," replied Chuck.

"Oh, goodie. So that bag of Crunchy Cockroach Corn Snacks hanging there is real," said Bruce, gazing up at a tree with a paper bag hanging off one of the branches. He sniffed it. "Yum," he said. "My favourite."

"Why would a bag of corn snacks be hanging from a tree?" asked Chuck.

"Maybe someone dropped it," said Bruce. "It'd be a shame to waste them though."

"Bruce, no!" cried Chuck.

But Chuck's words came too late. Bruce had already reached up and grabbed the bag. As he did, something white and gooey splatted all over his face. He looked up to see two bright green birds sitting on a branch above him.

“Hey, that’s disgust–” started Bruce, but before he could finish speaking, he fell to the ground, fast asleep.

“Get up, Bruce. It’s only a bit of bird poop,” said Jet.

Bruce didn’t respond.

“What’s the matter with him?” Jet asked.

“There must be something in the bird droppings,” said Chuck. “It’s another one of the Birdman’s tricks.”

“Terrific,” said Jet. “Now we’ll have to carry the big lump.”

Suddenly, the two birds swooped down from the trees and landed on Bruce's unconscious body.

"Hey, get away from him," said Jet, rushing towards Bruce. But he was not quick enough to prevent the birds lifting Bruce up and carrying him into the air.

"Bruce," yelled Jet.

Chuck and Jet watched helplessly as the birds carried off their friend. Had he been awake, Bruce would have easily sorted the birds out, but as it was, he was in no state to fight back at all.

"This is very bad," said Chuck. "Like the fan club of a pop group that has recently split up, we are rapidly losing members."

"When I catch up with that Birdman, I'll teach him to stick his beak into our business and make off with our friends," said Jet.

"This Birdman is a more cunning foe than we realized," said Chuck. "He must have identified Bruce's appetite as his weakness during our last encounter and then set this trap for him."

"It seems like those birds are taking him to the same place as Donnie," said Jet, checking the tracking device.

"We must continue with great caution," replied Chuck.

"I'll teach that no-good bird-brain a lesson he won't forget."

"Calm down, Jet," said Chuck. "We must

take control of this situation. We are already down to half our number because of this villain."

"Yeah, and I'll more than rattle his cage when I catch up with him," muttered Jet.

CHAPTER FIVE
SLOW-SINKING MUD

The condor carried Donnie high above the spectacular mountain range. With the blustery winds knocking him about, he was unable to reach his backpack or phone. Donnie was so frustrated that he even resorted to reasoning with the silent bird.

"If you let me go, I could introduce you to some very nice songbirds," he said. "Good looking bird like you, I could fix you up. I mean, it must get lonely up here."

But either it didn't understand or it wasn't listening.

On the other side of Mount Waytusteep, Donnie caught his first glimpse of the Forbidden Palace. It was a magnificent pyramid-like structure, made from enormous rectangular blocks. In the shadow of the great mountain, the palace was surrounded by a vast flat area of mud, with nothing but a few trees growing in it.

Remembering what Señor Citizen had said about the slow-sinking mud, Donnie very much hoped the condor wasn't about to drop him in it.

But no sooner had he thought this than the condor released him.

"Ahhh!" he cried as he plummeted down.

Donnie knew that if he landed straight in the mud, the force of the fall would ensure that he sunk like a stone. He reached for his gadget bag but, to his horror, he found it wasn't there. Turning, he saw that the condor had torn it from his back and dropped it separately. All Donnie had was a piece of rope from his parachute, which flapped uselessly behind him as he fell.

Focused on getting the bag, he put his arms to his side and angled his body towards it. He was almost within grabbing distance when a sudden gust of wind batted the bag away.

He was close to the ground now and there was no time to try getting the bag again. Instead he spotted a tree in the middle of the marsh and reached out to grab a branch.

"Got it," he exclaimed. But the branch snapped and came away in his hand.

He landed with a SQUELCH! Thankfully, the branch had slowed him down enough to prevent him from entirely disappearing beneath the swampy mud.

He watched his gadget bag land just out of reach and tried to move towards it, but the mud tightened its grip and pulled him downwards.

Donnie carefully tied the end of the rope into a lasso. His bag was sinking fast but so was he – he needed to save himself before he could rescue it. He threw the lasso over a sturdy-looking branch then hauled himself up on to the tree, out of the mud.

Finally he was safe, but he was also stuck. There was no way he could escape the marsh without his bag. He was about to retrieve it when he spotted two bright green birds fly over the marsh and drop something.

Donnie recognized the blue jumpsuit immediately. "Bruce," he yelled.

Bruce landed head first in the soft mud with an enormous splash. Judging by the lack of movement, Donnie realized that Bruce must be unconscious.

"Hey, Bruce," cried Donnie. "Look, there's a massive pot of gecko gizzards behind you." There was still no response.

"Wow, he must be properly out for the count if the promise of his favourite food doesn't even stir him."

Donnie threw the lasso expertly, hooking it around Bruce's leg. Then he pulled his unconscious friend towards him, straining under the effort. With Bruce's weight and the pull of the mud, it took all of his strength. "Come on, you great big lump," he shouted, as he finally dragged Bruce to safety.

He had rescued Bruce, but Donnie watched with dismay as his gadget bag disappeared into the mud. Gone forever.

In spite of the fresh mountain breeze, Jet was feeling anything but cool.

"This Birdman doesn't play fair," he said, furiously.

"When do the Ringmaster's recruits ever play fair?" replied Chuck.

"Yeah, but normally you can fight them," he replied. "This guy doesn't even show himself. As soon as I see him, I'll introduce him to some new moves I've been working on. Let's see, there's the Double Butterfly Pinch, the Angled Wheelbarrow Punch and the High-flying Chopstick Slap for starters. I'll Ninja-boom him all the way to—"

"You need to control yourself, Jet," interrupted Chuck. "Your anger will not help us."

"I'm just fed up with this guy making a

fool out of us."

"He is trying to give the Ringmaster time to reach the Forbidden Palace before us," said Chuck.

"Well, I'll make him regret ever leaving his nest when I catch up with him," threatened Jet.

"I suggest you find your inner calm immediately, Jet. You do not want to be so furious when you face this Birdman. And look! If I'm not mistaken, that opportunity may arise sooner than you think."

Ahead, the trail led to a rickety rope bridge that crossed a lush green valley. In the middle of the bridge stood a figure in a feathered cloak with his arms outstretched, standing absolutely still. His face was obscured by his hood, but his cloak and the three birds that hovered above him left Jet in no doubt as to who it was.

"The Birdman," he muttered. Jet drew his nunchucks and stepped on to the bridge. "Leave him to me."

"Wait, Jet. We must act tactically," said Chuck. "We have already seen how devious this villain is."

"Yeah, well, now he'll see how tough I am," said Jet dismissively. "Finally ready for a fair fight, are you, flappy features?" he shouted at the Birdman.

The Birdman did not reply. He didn't move at all.

"He's goading you," said Chuck. "He wants you to come to him."

"Then he's going to get what he wants," replied Jet.

"Please calm yourself," said Chuck.

"Calm myself?" exploded Jet. "Because of him we've lost Donnie and Bruce."

"Don't you see?" said Chuck. "This Birdman identifies the weakness in his enemy and uses it against them."

"Weakness?" scoffed Jet. "Jet Flashfeet doesn't have any weaknesses."

"We all have weaknesses," said Chuck. "And he knows that you are desperate for a direct fight."

"That's right," said Jet. "And he'll regret

ever setting foot on this bridge."

"The Way of the Scorpion teaches us–" began Chuck, but Jet wasn't listening.

"I don't care," he snapped. "I'm going to take him down."

Jet ran across the bridge towards the Birdman. "Come on, then," he cried. "Put up your wings and we'll see what you're made of."

The Birdman said nothing, but the feathers of his cloak shook in the breeze.

"He's quivering with fear," said Jet. "And so he should be. Ninja-boom!"

Jet leaped up and spun round, executing a magnificent roundhouse kick that should have sent the Birdman flying but instead failed to connect. Jet sank into the material of the Birdman's cloak, sending feathers flying everywhere.

As Jet landed on the cloak, the birds

twisted it around in the air, wrapping Jet inside. What Jet had taken to be the Birdman was actually just his cloak. The birds weren't hovering above – they were holding it up.

Before Jet had time to understand what was going on, he was caught up inside the cloak and being carried off by the birds, leaving Chuck behind.

CHAPTER SIX

CHUCK'S CHOICE

Chuck could do nothing but continue on the trek alone with his sword drawn, his brow furrowed and his mind focused. He tried to banish all emotions from his thoughts but it was no easy task. The Birdman had identified the weakness of every other member of the Clan and used it in order to get the better of them. His condor had snatched Donnie while he was occupied by his gadgets, he had used Bruce's appetite against him and Jet's desire to fight had been his downfall.

Chuck knew he would have to remain calm to defeat such a cunning enemy.

It took another couple of hours to reach Mount Waytusteep. The mountain loomed above Chuck and he understood how the palace had remained undiscovered for so long, tucked away behind it. In front of him was the passageway through the centre of Mount Waytusteep. Around him were great boulders freshly fallen from the recent earthquake.

Quickly, Chuck entered the passageway and made his way through the dark tunnel, remaining ever ready in case of ambush. But none came and, eventually, he reached the other side, where the mountain cast a great shadow and he could see the Forbidden Palace. The only way to get to the huge entrance of the palace was across a stone path over the muddy swamps that surrounded it. However, in the middle of the path stood the Birdman, with the condor resting on his arm.

"And so it is my turn to face this villain," muttered Chuck under his breath.

He made his way across the stones, keeping his eyes on the Birdman. No doubt he had a plan, but what weakness had he identified in Chuck?

As Chuck got nearer, he could see the Birdman's beady eyes. On the far side of the valley, bright sunlight was creeping towards the palace as the sun rose in the sky.

"*He who seeks Ultimate Power must sit upon the golden throne, so when the sun shines upon him, the earth shall be his own,*" said Chuck, remembering the rhyme. "Ah, now I understand. When the sun reaches a certain point in the sky, it will illuminate the palace. If the Ringmaster is on the throne when the sunlight hits it, he will gain Ultimate Power."

The Birdman nodded.

"Except that the Clan of the Scorpion are here to stop him," said Chuck. "Now, what did you do with the others?"

The Birdman raised his arm and pointed at a tree that stood in the centre of the marshy land around the palace. There, sitting in the tree's branches, were Bruce, Donnie and Jet.

When Chuck turned back to the Birdman, he was already walking towards the palace.

"What? You have no challenge for me?" said Chuck.

The Birdman ignored him and continued walking.

"Jet, Bruce, Donnie," shouted Chuck.

"Hey, Chuck," they yelled back.

"Do you have any way off that tree?" shouted Chuck.

"No. We're stuck," replied Bruce.

"What about Donnie's gadgets?" asked Chuck.

"Sunk in the mud," replied Donnie. "However, I do have an idea now you're here. I need you to collect two handfuls of pebbles, some tree bark and seventeen bendy branches."

Chuck was about to do as Donnie said when he stopped in his tracks. Suddenly, he understood why the Birdman hadn't attempted to stop him, instead simply pointing to his friends. The Birdman had identified his weakness.

"Sorry. I'm afraid you'll have to find a way out of the swamp by yourselves," shouted Chuck.

"What?" replied the others.

"The Birdman knows that my loyalty to the Clan of the Scorpion is my weakness. He knows my first instinct will be to rescue you, but if I do that it will be too late. The sun is moving to its highest point in the sky. Soon it will shine down into the palace. Then all will be lost."

"So, you're going to go in on your own?" asked Donnie.

"Yes," said Chuck. "But I believe you will

find a way to escape without my assistance. You see, the Birdman is wrong. My weakness is not my reliance on you. My strength is my faith in you."

"But it's impossible to get off this tree," said Bruce.

"As a good friend of ours says, when one is truly in touch with one's inner ninja, impossible ceases to exist," said Chuck. "Good luck."

Chuck turned and ran towards the palace.

Jet, Donnie and Bruce looked at each other, stunned.

"The next time I see that Birdman I'll snap his beak off," said Bruce.

"Yeah, and that condor is on a flight path to pain," said Donnie.

"Flight..." said Jet. "Hold on. What did Chuck just say?"

"He said we'd have to figure out our

own way off this tree," replied Bruce.

"No, he said that when one is in touch with one's inner ninja, impossible ceases to exist. That's what Grandmaster One-Eye said about the Flight of Enlightenment."

"Not *that* again," said Donnie.

"It's our only chance. The palace is further than any of us can jump, but with the Flight of Enlightenment we could get there. Come on, get into position."

All three of them manoeuvred into a cross-legged position, facing the palace.

"Now, close your eyes," said Jet. "Imagine you are standing in front of those doors. Imagine bursting through and taking on the circus goons. Imagine defeating the Ringmaster. Nothing could be simpler. We can be there in the blink of an eye. Now, slowly, breathing deeply, on my count. One... Two... Three..."

Jet, Donnie and Bruce pushed down on the trunk and all three meerkats went flying forward.

CHAPTER SEVEN

BIRD STRIKE!

Chuck ruled out trying to enter the palace through the huge front doors. He knew that the circus goons would be expecting that. Instead he clambered up the side of the palace, leaping from stone to stone with ease. Chuck had worked out that for the sunlight to shine on to the throne inside the palace, there must be an opening in the top of the palace.

When he reached the top he saw he was right. As he had expected, the hole wasn't very large, meaning he could easily cover it with his body in order to prevent the sun from shining in and illuminating the throne.

However, as he poked his head over the hole he heard the whistling of a knife flying straight at him. Anyone with slower reactions would have been skewered, but Chuck's instincts were as sharp as the knife itself and he dodged the blade.

"Das meerkatzchen is on the roof," cried Herr Flick, sending another knife his way.

"You can't win, Ringmaster," shouted Chuck.

"Really, Mr Cobracrusher?" The Ringmaster's voice echoed off the walls. "By now you'll have realized that when the sunlight reaches that hole and illuminates this throne, I will gain Ultimate Power. I imagine your plan is to block the hole, of course, but the clowns' cake guns would blast through anything you could place over the top. Perhaps you are contemplating leaping through it. Even if you manage to avoid Herr Flick's knives and Sheffield and Grimsby's guns, it would be you against all of us. One against six. Not good odds. You're a great leader, Chuck, but what is a leader with no one to lead?"

"Just an 'er'," said Grimsby.

The circus troupe laughed at this terrible joke, but their hoots died away when they heard a bang from the other side of the palace.

"What was that?" demanded the Ringmaster.

Knowing that the circus goons would only be distracted momentarily, Chuck took the opportunity. He somersaulted up and dived through the hole, drawing his sword as he flew down towards the Ringmaster, who was sitting on the throne. Behind the Ringmaster stood the Birdman, his feathered hood over his head and a huge condor on his shoulder.

Chuck dodged the knives and cake-gun blasts, and landed into a roll. He was almost upon the Ringmaster when Doris hit him with a mid-air pirouette that sent him flying off course.

"Good dog," said the Ringmaster. "Keep him busy. It won't be long now."

Chuck stood face to face with the snarling poodle. But before either of them could make a move, there was a second bang and the huge doors to the hall swung open with a cry of "Bruce Force!"

As the dust settled, three figures were revealed in the doorway.

"Hi, Chuck. We thought you might like some help," said Jet.

"Hey, everyone looks surprised to see us," said Donnie. "Perhaps we should have knocked."

"I did knock," said Bruce. "Well, I *knocked* the doors off their hinges."

"You interfering little meerkats," snarled the Ringmaster. "Always trying to get in my way, but not this time. Circus goons, keep them at bay and we will still have the last laugh."

"You got it, boss," said Grimsby.

"Let's bake," said Sheffield.

Both clowns started firing at the meerkats, while Herr Flick threw knives and Doris attacked Chuck.

"Before us each enemy cowers, for now we fight until victory is ours," said Chuck, jumping into action.

"Jet, you deal with Herr Flick," said Donnie. "Bruce and I will get the clowns."

"You got it," said Jet.

Donnie and Bruce ran full pelt towards the clowns. Each time they hit Bruce with the quick-setting cake-mix, he burst through with a cry of "Bruce Force!"

Donnie zigzagged to avoid being hit, then ran straight under Grimsby's legs.

Grimsby spun round to get him. "Where did he go?" he asked, puzzled.

"Behind you," said Donnie.

The sad-faced clown turned and fired, but Donnie wasn't there, and the stream of cake mixture hit Sheffield's leg instead.

"Sorry," shouted Grimsby.

Donnie, who had been clinging to Grimsby's back, somersaulted over him, landed on the barrel of his gun and knocked it out of his hands. He grabbed the gun and turned it on the clowns.

"You clowns should know how to take a cake in the face," said Donnie, squeezing the trigger.

As the gooey mixture splatted against his face, Grimsby staggered back and collided with Sheffield. They both tumbled and fell.

Bruce grabbed Sheffield's gun and the two meerkats fired repeatedly, until the clowns were lost in a mass of expanding cake mix.

"Anyone for clown cake?" asked Donnie.

"Even *I* wouldn't eat that," said Bruce.

"Why not?" asked Donnie.

"I reckon it would taste funny," he replied.

On the other side of the palace, Jet avoided every one of Herr Flick's deadly knives, before landing a powerful punch on his chest, sending him flying backwards. Meanwhile, Chuck wrestled Doris to the ground and pinned her down.

"Your victory will be short-lived," cried the Ringmaster. "The sun is almost upon us."

The sun had finally come over the mountain top and a ray of light was shining through the hole, slowly moving towards the throne.

"And now, ladies and gentlemen, boys and girls, let me introduce to you, the latest addition to my circus ... the Birdman of Cusco."

The Birdman stepped forward and the condor flapped its wings menacingly.

"We'll bring these feathered fiends down to earth with a bump," sneered Jet.

The Birdman pulled out a whistle and made a high-pitched sound. Suddenly, hundreds of birds flocked into the palace through the doors and the roof. Red, green, blue, small and large. The birds all hurtled towards a single target – the meerkats.

The Birdman seemed to be issuing instructions using the whistle, sending the birds at the Clan of the Scorpion in organized attack formations. Above the flapping and squawking, the sound of the Ringmaster's maniacal laughter could be heard.

CHAPTER EIGHT

AIR FORCE

As battalions of birds swooped down, Chuck stood on his hind legs and swung his sword to keep them at bay. Jet dived out of the way of a pair of birds so they ended up jabbing each other with their sharp beaks. An eagle attempted to grab Bruce with its huge talons, but he brought it down with a mighty blow.

Donnie brought yet more birds crashing down to earth using the clowns' cake guns. "Bird pie, anyone?" he cried.

Bruce spotted the Birdman's condor

across the hall. “I’ll teach that jumped-up pigeon to mess with us,” he muttered.

Bruce charged forward and leaped up. Then he grabbed the bird’s feet, dragging it to the ground and giving it such a pounding that feathers flew everywhere. The bird squawked wildly and desperately tried to get away, but Bruce was holding on fast. Before long he was swinging it round and round, bashing any other birds that got near.

"Time to fly," Bruce said, suddenly releasing the condor and sending it hurtling across the palace into a pillar, where it finally collapsed to the ground in a heap of feathers.

The Birdman still stood beside the throne, giving orders to the birds with a series of toots from his whistle.

"Jet," called Chuck. "If you get the whistle, he won't be able to control the birds."

"I'm on it," replied Jet. He ran across the hall, then sprang up at the Birdman, aiming a kick at his head.

However, the feathered fiend had seen him coming and dodged out of the way.

"Ha, the Birdman is too fast for you, Flashfeet," said the Ringmaster, observing the action from his throne.

"That's what you think," replied Jet.

As the Birdman went to blow his whistle, Jet leaped up and kicked it out of his mouth, sending it spinning across the floor.

"Doris, fetch that whistle," cried the Ringmaster.

As Doris ran after it, Jet executed a perfect scissor kick that sent the Birdman flying.

Jet knocked the Birdman back so hard that he bounced between two pillars like a pinball and collapsed to the ground, feathers fluttering around him.

"Ninja-plume!" cried Jet.

Without anyone to give them instructions, the birds retreated to the roof of the palace.

Chuck turned to the Ringmaster. "The game's up, Ringmaster," he said.

"You mean the game's up for *you*," replied the Ringmaster. "Because here comes the sun."

The bright yellow sunlight streamed down through the hole in the roof, hitting the golden throne and bouncing beams of light all around the hall.

"Finally," cried the Ringmaster. "I will have Ultimate Power. The world shall be mine!"

The meerkats, the circus goons and the birds waited to see what would happen next.

Nothing happened.

"So, what now?" asked Grimsby.

"I expect it's made him invincible... Or maybe he can shoot out laser beams from his eyes or something..." Sheffield looked at his boss uncertainly. "Boss?"

But the Ringmaster seemed equally confused about what, if anything, had happened.

Chuck looked around. "The brother who built this palace was a great engineer, but he wasn't a magician," he muttered, recalling what Señor Citizen had said.

A great rumbling came from underneath and the ground began to shake.

"I've got it!" shouted Chuck. "I understand the meaning of the riddle in the scroll. We need to get out, right now."

"You fools! You cannot escape me," said the Ringmaster.

"This palace isn't what you think it is," replied Chuck. "The man who built the palace hated the king's desire for Ultimate Power. He *hid* the palace from the king. So, why did he build it at all?"

"Well?" demanded the Ringmaster impatiently. "What's the answer?"

"It's a trap for people like you," said Chuck.

They felt another almighty tremor rock the palace walls.

"But the scroll says the world shall be my own," protested the Ringmaster.

"Not the world. The *earth*. When the sun shines on him *the earth* shall be his own," said Chuck. "The earth will be your own. It will be the only thing you've got, when it has swallowed you up."

"Of course," said Donnie. "This place isn't magic at all. It's all engineering. By sitting on the throne when the sun shines upon it, you have triggered a mechanism that causes this entire palace to collapse!"

A huge piece of stone from the roof crashed down to the ground close to Chuck, and he dived to safety from the shower of rubble that followed it.

More pieces of the palace came crashing down, blocking the huge doorway.

"Someone do something," ordered the Ringmaster, at last standing up from the throne with a panicked look on his face.

"Don't look at us," said Grimsby, who was still attached to Sheffield in a mass of solid cake mix.

"You half-baked idiots!" shouted the Ringmaster.

Doris barked loudly. She ran over to the Birdman, who was still recovering from his encounter with the pillars. She dropped the whistle into his hand and barked at him until he stirred.

"Yes, Doris. The Birdman can get us out of here," yelled the Ringmaster.

The Birdman nodded silently and blew his whistle several times.

The dishevelled condor flew to his master, grabbed his cloak with its talons and raised him into the air as the temple rocked from side to side.

"What about the rest of us?" shouted the Ringmaster.

The Birdman blew the whistle again and more birds swooped down from the ceiling to pick up the others. It took over twenty birds to raise the clowns, but soon all the circus goons were being lifted out of the collapsing palace.

"Maybe I didn't succeed," cried the Ringmaster, "but you meerkats will die here. Goodbye, Clan of the Scorpion!"

The meerkats watched helplessly as their enemies were carried out to safety.

"Donnie, how can we get out?" asked Chuck, diving out of the way of a huge stone pillar that came crashing down.

"If I had my gadget bag..." Donnie began.

"We need to think of something quickly, otherwise we're all going underground," said Jet.

The ground shifted beneath their feet and the golden throne rocked back and forth.

"I've got an idea," said Donnie. "Bruce, roll that pillar up behind the throne."

"Sure," replied Bruce. He ran over and, with astonishing ease, rolled the huge pillar over the unstable stone floor.

"Now, Jet, one of your cannon kicks to that throne should knock it over."

Without a word, Jet kicked the throne. It was extremely heavy, but Jet's powerful kick knocked it back so it landed on top of the pillar.

"Now, everyone climb on," said Donnie, clambering up the back of the throne.

"Hey, it looks like a seesaw," said Bruce.

"Exactly. We're about to seesaw out of here," said Donnie. "Get ready."

One of the huge rocks from the roof came crashing down on the other side of the throne, flinging the meerkats up into the air.

"Ninja-booooom!" cried Jet as they were projected up and out of the top of the crumbling palace.

They flew through the air and landed in a heap near the palace entrance, which was now just a heap of stones.

They picked themselves up and dashed

across the stone path through the mud. Even the path was sinking down into the swamp. The meerkats ran at breakneck speed to avoid going down with it.

When they reached the solid ground, they stopped and turned to watch the final bits of the palace collapse.

Chuck looked over to where the Ringmaster and his troupe were being carried off by the flock of birds. "Yet again our enemy has escaped," he said.

"I can't believe we got out," said Bruce.

"Yes, well done, Donnie," said Chuck. "And all without your gadget bag. You see, our best weapons truly do come from within."

"Where did you get the idea to use the throne as a seesaw?" asked Jet.

"It suddenly hit me that what we needed was to be thrown out," said Donnie. "And what better to be *thrown* by than a *throne*?"

The others groaned.

"Donnie, your quick thinking saved us today," said Chuck, "but I fear nothing will save us from your terrible puns."

OUT NOW!

SMALL. FURRY. DEADLY.
NINJA MEERKATS
THE CLAN OF THE SCORPION
GARETH P. JONES

SMALL. FURRY. DEADLY.
NINJA MEERKATS
THE EYE OF THE MONKEY
GARETH P. JONES

SMALL. FURRY. DEADLY.
NINJA MEERKATS
ESCAPE FROM ICE MOUNTAIN
GARETH P. JONES

SMALL. FURRY. DEADLY.
NINJA MEERKATS
HOLLYWOOD SHOWDOWN
GARETH P. JONES